MRS. WISHY-WASHY'S FARM

MRS. WISHY-WASHY'S FARM

Joy Cowley   illustrated by **Elizabeth Fuller**

PHILOMEL BOOKS

This is Mrs. Wishy-Washy
and this is her farm.

Here is her house
and her truck and her barn.

Here by the barn is the old tin tub
where all the animals go for a scrub.

Wishy-washy. Wishy-washy.
"Moo!" the cow cries.
"I hate this old tub!
I've got soap in my eyes."

Wishy-washy. Wishy-washy.
"Ee-ee!" the pig squeals.
"I have been scrubbed
from my nose to my heels."

Wishy-washy. Wishy-washy.
"Quack!" the duck moans.
"I've got suds in my feathers
and aches in my bones."

The scrubbing is over. The tub goes away.
"No more washing!" the animals say.

"Moo-moo!"

"Ee-ee!"

"Quack, quack, quack!"

"Bye, Mrs. Wishy-Washy,
mean old Mrs. Wishy-Washy.
We are leaving you
and we won't be back."

Fast down the highway,
they run side by side.
Where will they go?
Where will they hide?

"Ee-ee! The city!"
squeals the old pig.
"We'll go to the city
where the barns are big."

But the city is as wild
as a farm stampede.

There is nowhere to rest
and nowhere to feed.

The three hungry animals
walk into a barn.
There is food on the dishes,
but it's not like the farm!

The cow looks around
with an anxious face.
"I think we could be
in the wrong eating place."

Along comes the cook
with an angry shout.
"You'll be roast on toast
if you don't get out!"

They run for their lives
to the barn next door

and find themselves in
a hardware store. Oops!

Then a van pulls up
in two shakes of a tail.
It's the pick-up van
from the animal jail.

They're taken away!
Oh, what bad luck
for the cow and the pig
and the poor old duck!

They sit in a huddle,
hungry and pale,
in the cold, muddy cage
of the animal jail.

Then the unhappy cow
and the pig and the duck
hear the chug-chug-chug
of the old farm truck.

They moo and they squeal,
they quack and they cheer.

"It's dear Mrs. Wishy-Washy.
She is here!"

Far from the city and back on the farm,
the animals run to the old red barn.

Now Mrs. Wishy-Washy fills up the tub.
"Come on, you three!
You need a good scrub."

"Oh, bliss!" says the cow,
and she jumps right in.

"Oh, bliss!" says the pig
with a happy grin.

"Oh, bliss!" says the duck,
splashing in with the rest.
"There's no doubt about it.
Home is best!"

Wishy-washy.

Wishy-washy.

PATRICIA LEE GAUCH, EDITOR

Philomel Books,
a division of Penguin Young Readers Group,
345 Hudson Street, New York, NY 10014.
Philomel Books, Reg. U.S. Pat. & Tm. Off. Published simultaneously in Canada.
Manufactured in China by South China Printing Co. Ltd.

Designed by Semadar Megged
Text set in 19-point AvantGarde Demi
The art was done in watercolor and ink on watercolor paper

Library of Congress Cataloging-in-Publication Data
Cowley, Joy. Mrs. Wishy-Washy's Farm / Joy Cowley ; illustrated by Elizabeth Fuller ;
Patricia Lee Gauch, editor.
p. cm.
Summary: Tired of being washed by Mrs. Wishy-Washy, a cow, pig,
and duck leave her farm and head for the city.
[1. Farm life—Fiction. 2. Cows—Fiction. 3. Pigs—Fiction. 4. Ducks—Fiction. 5. Stories in rhyme.] I. Fuller,
Elizabeth, ill. II. Gauch, Patricia Lee, ed. III. Title.
PZ8.3.C8345 Wi 2003   [E]—dc21   2002001257
ISBN 0-399-23872-7
5 7 9 10 8 6